Sarah's Sleepover

by Bobbie Rodriguez
illustrated by Mark Graham

Viking

VIKING
Published by the Penguin Group
Penguin Putnam Books for Young Readers, 345 Hudson Street, New York, New York 10014, U.S.A.
Penguin Books Ltd, 27 Wrights Lane, London W8 5TZ, England
Penguin Books Australia Ltd, Ringwood, Victoria, Australia
Penguin Books Canada Ltd, 10 Alcorn Avenue, Toronto, Ontario, Canada M4V 3B2
Penguin Books (N.Z.) Ltd, 182-190 Wairau Road, Auckland 10, New Zealand

Penguin Books Ltd, Registered Offices: Harmondsworth, Middlesex, England

First published in 2000 by Viking, a division of Penguin Putnam Books for Young Readers.

1 3 5 7 9 10 8 6 4 2

LIBRARY OF CONGRESS CATALOGING-IN-PUBLICATION DATA
Rodriguez, Bobbie.
Sarah's sleepover / by Bobbie Rodriguez ; illustrated by Mark Graham.
p. cm.
Summary: When the lights go out while her cousins are spending the
night, a young blind girl shows them what to do in the dark.
ISBN 0-670-87750-6 (hc.)
[1. Sleepovers Fiction. 2. Blind Fiction. 3. Physically
handicapped Fiction. 4. Cousins Fiction.] I. Graham, Mark, date-
ill. II. Title.
PZ7.R1883Sar 2000 [Fic]—DC21 99-32058 CIP

Printed in Hong Kong
Set in Janson Text

The writing of this book would never have been possible without the support of Regina Hayes, Brian Stanton, and my better half and best friend, Brian Bannerman.
—B.R.

To Furball
—M.G.

"Here they come!" Sarah shouted.

"Are you sure?" Mama asked.

Sarah *was* sure. She could always hear the cars coming before anyone else. Sarah had been counting the days until her favorite weekend. "Sleepover weekend" was when all her cousins came to stay at the farm.

The line of cars and trucks pulled up in front of the house. The door flew open, and in came Sarah's aunts, uncles, and cousins.

"Yippie!" Molly shouted. "Look at all this snow!" Sarah couldn't see Molly, but she could recognize her voice anywhere. Sarah knew Jessica, Katie, Amy, and Lisa were there, too. They didn't have to shout like Molly. She knew them by their footsteps.

The girls started hugging and jumping up and down.

"Let's go play some games," said Katie.

"Yes, let's!" the other girls agreed.

"Mama, may we go upstairs to my room to play?" asked Sarah.

"Certainly," said Mama. "But first, get some hot chocolate. Grandma made some just for you ladies." The girls lined up to get their hot chocolate and started up the stairs. Sarah was the last to get to her room. She was always careful on the stairs. Sometimes people would accidentally leave things she could trip over.

Jessica yelled, "Let's play checkers!"

"No, silly," said Amy. "Sarah can't play that. She can't see the game board."

"Okay," Molly said, "let's play musical chairs."

"I can't play that either," said Sarah, feeling bad.

"I know," Lisa said. "Let's make up funny songs." So that's what they did.

They were laughing so loud Mama had to call up the stairs twice before they heard her.

"Girls! We are going up the road to visit the Higgins. We won't be gone long. The phone number is right here if you need anything."

"Oh boy! We're finally big enough to be left alone!" said Amy as she bopped Katie on the head with a pillow. They all started laughing and throwing pillows. The louder they laughed the better Sarah's aim became.

Just then the wind howled, and the lights blinked and then went out.
"Oh no," yelled Katie as she spilled her hot cocoa.
"Uh oh," said Molly as she knocked Sarah's lamp off her desk.
"This is really scary!" they agreed.
Sarah had no idea why everybody suddenly seemed so clumsy. "What's the matter?" she asked.
"The lights went out!" Molly answered.

Katie clicked the light switch, but nothing happened.

"That's all right," Sarah said. "You don't have to be scared. I know my way around in the dark. I do it all the time. Let's hold hands and go downstairs to call Mama; I know the Higgins' number. And we can get some snacks while we're there."

"Okay," the girls said. They lined up single file, and down the stairs they went without a trip, bang, or crash.

While Jessica made the call, Sarah started pulling out bags of chips and cookies from the cupboard.

Suddenly from outside they heard a *Whooo! Whooo! Whooo!*

The girls shrieked. "What was that?"

"Just our old barn owl," said Sarah. "I call him Barney."

Then, as they were tucking goodies under their arms, they heard *Owoooo! Owoooo! Owoooo!*

"Yipes! What was that?" asked Amy.

"Don't be scared," said Sarah. "That's just a coyote. They don't hurt people. They're real scaredy-cats."

"Let's go back upstairs," said Molly. "Sarah, you lead the way. We'll hold on to you."

Back in Sarah's room Katie had a good idea. "Let's tell ghost stories."

"Okay," said Amy. "I'll go first. Once there was a girl who lived in a pumpkin patch. She had seeds for eyes and leaves for hair. One dark and foggy night, all that could be heard from the pumpkin patch was—"

Thump, thump, thump.

"*What was that?*" the girls shrieked.

Sarah squeaked, "I don't know!"

"Girls, we're back," Mama said, standing in the doorway. The girls laughed so hard they rolled around on the floor. "I didn't know I was so funny!"

That made the girls laugh even harder. "I came up to tell you that Sarah's papa fixed the broken fuse." Sarah's mother flipped the light switch.

"No, turn them off! Turn them off! We're having much more fun in the dark!" they pleaded. So Mama did just that on her way downstairs to join the other grownups.

The girls continued to play in the dark.
They hummed songs and guessed the titles.
They told stories. They sniffed all the cookies
and guessed which ones were chocolate. And
no one knew how Amy's smelly gym sock
found its way onto the cookie plate!

At last everyone but Sarah fell asleep. Sarah smiled to herself as she thought over all that had happened that evening. She knew this was going to be the best sleepover weekend ever!